SKYLIGHTS

ADAM CHRISTOPHER MOORHEAD

ISBN 978-1-959182-92-4 (paperback)
ISBN 978-1-959182-93-1 (digital)

Rushmore Press LLC
1 800 460 9188
www.rushmorepress.com

Printed in the United States of America

Hope for Us

Fog and mist . . .
Puddle on the path
Leading from the street to drain.
Wind and water, dimmed day's light,
Sun fading in hindsight.
I stare at the ocean, toward its path
Beyond the streetlights
Past electric
To the ocean and the waves.
Tossed and turned from today,
This point on the earth is upset
But I am not.
Streets battered with water,
Yet they remain.
It's so hard to see.
How am I still here?
Where you might still be . . .
I am stilled with hope for us.

Jamal

If you have something, say it
If you go away, leave it
But don't leave me back there
All alone
If you go away, take it
And you might as well make it
Just don't let me fake it
I ask of you
Do the words fit, Jamal?
I feel it in my bones
I feel it in my sleep
I am so much like you
Here for you too
Don't worry, not leaving you
I am so much like you
I wish we were more the same
I am going nowhere
Staying right here for you
I am so much like you
I wish we were more the same

Witness Light Fall

When I give you all of my time
Shout out these words for you
Lift up a cry to bless you
And you never hear or see
You only want to witness to me
What do I do? What do I say? How do I see?

With all my words poured out
Nothing left to dismiss
I lift up a cry for you
And you never hear or see
How can I still be
With love? In mercy? With life?

Stand here and be counted
Sorrow goes away
I hear and receive
Your light fall my way

Don't go headed sideways
Head up to the mountain
Be washed in the light
Until somewhere else we can go

Curve

Sound it out
Play it loud
Every word and rhythm
There's a curve ahead
Don't be led
To think you can swerve it
Believe in love
That is your job
Every second and minute
Forget the noise
Among all the choices
Stay with me forever
I hear your sound
I hear your victory

New Harmony

Dear relevant, what do you want?
Dear relative, what do I give?
Dear relevant, what do you want from me?
Dear relevant, have mercy on me
I will sound it out
Tone and rhythm
It is what I can do
Turn it up for you
Make it loud for you
Take what you hear
From us to there
Drum with it every moment
In all the down times
In the tough memories
Let it sound and lift you up
Light up your room
It may be midnight where you are
It is still warm I hope
I won't forget your walls and your ways
Of history when I was not a thought
In my mother's life, in my mother's arms
Holy Mary, hear
A new harmony's cry for heaven
To be set apart and to be free

Fog Inside-Out

Today, I rise
After little rest
Should I return to sleep?
Pull up with the day
Outside still dark
Barely a sunrise
Fog at eye level, fog overhead
I press out of bed
Through the rest of the home
And go out
To the fog that awaits
Crying out a warning
For another day
Of good old grumblings
No sun, at least not yet
Only fog, cloud, tired, slow
Heavy is my head
With nothing more than needs
For rest and renewal
I walk a mile with the fog
Only to return back to home
And back to bed
But at least not yet
The day is still
I am always looking ahead at tomorrow's rest
I believe I will use today to sleep on
Until the fog is still no more

From a Dream

Dreams long ago
Can still be held
Ever lightly so
A lost love can be found
An even better falling
For someone you honor
And hold to the highest esteem
A romance sustained
In troubled times, simplicity
Instead of complex
No hurry
Your pace, not mine
An exercise that's astounding
A newness, exhilarate
When the world seems right today
Not just one day, but every day
Between the two who can't get enough
Of the level of trust between earth and heaven

Royalty

Royalty: let me be
Feast for a while
Serve: trust me I will
Ready for your smile
For a time and for a while
Grant me a chance
To give you the best
Wailing to the tune
You know how to show my better half
I walk on and on
So I can get on with my better days
What will transcend between us
From so many years of the same old stuff?
I will be the gentleman
Hold the door, be all the peaceful
Among everyone else
Throw me in the water
Dance while we ascend the mountain
And I will bask in the glow of the starlight
Hanging on by midnight
Hurry up now

Trains

Hey there
Standing, looking over straight at me
There's something happening
I wonder if you actually see
This is a place that holds
All shapes and kinds of freedom
Now we have the ball, let's take advantage and run
Woah, there is something I've got to tell you
Something's been tripping on my mind way too long
Tomorrow, we are leaving, taking separate trains home
This happy feeling has a side that just seems wrong
We've had our great good times
Never thought they would ever come to pass
Even from day one, you know time has gone away so fast
Strange how you meet somebody
Not sure, but you know the feeling is good
Even when no words are said
You are confident that you're understood
I've got to get on with my life
And you've got to get on with yours
It was something we've said, but sometimes, it just feels like more

Schooled

Write it out and tell somebody
Put it down and be still for once
Take a moment would you, sir?
Would love to help you out if I could
I can only go with you so far
Fame, you sure about it?
Friends, great to have them if you could
Go with the ones you have
Try not to turn them loose
I remember the gray and lights
Days when only music made sense
Contentment, life as is
Nothing more, nothing nevertheless
You aren't guaranteed tomorrow
You do not have anything to prove
To anyone anymore
Not always so happy
More thankful, grateful, content
Until you start to believe it could be
Much easier and better
Make room for the creative, expressive with respect

Sky

If I tend to push the limit
If I'm honest
If we are breakable like glass
Why do I always have to push?
Why do I always want to test it?
Truth: I am a miracle mess
Growing, learning, not looking back
Not to admit I feel sad some days
You can only offer
But to have no one is possible
Everyone has friends, right?
Best friends forever and ever
A good friend saves you from what comes out
So from now on when I speak
I will watch the words
When I laugh I will consider why
If I can be happy and in love and someone else can't
Maybe I should listen to them
For what do I miss but everything
I need the love over space
Bigger than every morning sky;
A rock show
A drive-thru
It's just what I needed to do
Sky was dimming down
But I remember what you said
Or was it how you were able to listen
I forget
Something about the extraordinary
Without total knowledge

Without your eyes
Without physics
Without needing to solve
You just like it
Cause and effect where you like it
So much that you might turn to need it
And then you give in to falling reckless
And self is lost
Or you feel weak, checkmated
I am at a loss bigger than the skies above
I guess I could learn
I guess I could use more experience
In looking out beyond
And not fearing so much
What do they say about us?
If they say bad things, I should work harder
For their mercy
Not everyone will ask us to stay
Not everyone will even say hello
Nor even give a hug
I don't live in the past
I don't look back
But only for a sense of victory
When not in the spotlight
Especially if I run from the homeless
Beneath a dark blue sky

Running Energy Gone

Down below where the river runs
Where we grew up
Full of energy and go
Set up a stage and played
Maybe twice the same four tunes
After a brief hiatus, starting to slow on down
Here we are again, where we started out
Musically that is
J-ville and G-ville, or somewhere in between
Pushing all the paperwork, still listening
To the same old stuff
To the same old stuff
I'm more southern
Others more Cali west-coast
Still others love the classic rock
And the last one always wants the pop
No schedule anymore
Nowhere to be every day
At least not yet and for now.
Where we came from
We were all launched into
The great unknown of graduation
Praise graduation
We were ready to hit it up and head it out
And we did
Never going back
But playing on and on
The same way we did before
The running energy was gone
Too many questions for space and time

Keep on running my friend
Have a blast going where
The water runs cold
Where you can have a little more fun
Before the running energy is gone

Heavy Home

Heavenly thunder
Loud
Weather filled with dropping footsteps
Run for cover, is this a theater?
From only the weather?
Run from the cold and the rain

You believed you could handle it
But you got stuck
Too far away from home
The shelter that provides
Freedom took you too far
But you can always find a way
Home if you would

It may take a while
You may be disturbed
During these days of venture
Like a pattern
Venture only to return again
Home
It is important

Been away for too long it seems
You know things aren't the same
Some things must change
It's not an option
I don't owe you
You don't owe me
Keep your return to home in sight

Our Ceaseless Quarrel

It hurts when we quarrel
And nothing seems to change
Like two boxers in unending rematches
With unending rounds until knockout
How did we start into this?
I messed up, I was late
I did not care either
Our timing does not agree
Is that it for our fellowship?
It seems you are never afraid
To yell at the ones you care about the most
And it hurts
It hurts them, it hurts you
How do you get out of all of this?
Should we just leave
Gamble away our quarrel
Only to return next time even worse?
Space
Time to slow down, cool off, repent
When can we all get along again?
We forgive but only hope to forget
Forgiving is never cheap
And we don't always
But someone does, someone has to
If it is me, I will not grow calloused
I will stay sensitive
Not invade
For the sake of our love

Never Leave You

All over the place
Don't want to worry
About tomorrow
Where will I stay?
What will we eat?

Am I going to be rich?
Do I know where to go?
What about the guy with a sign?
God help us

Be able to talk
At very least if they ask
And they will, so prepare yourself
Know how to sound and get ready

This is my life song, my preacher's sound
This is my fight song, lay myself down

You keep talking and I won't listen
What in the world?
I have not forgotten you, I promise
Too soft to forget you

Good-hearted that seems to mess up a lot
And with a mind of my own, so screw it
Without anyone else
Maybe I should stop and let you know
Maybe I need to let you in for once
But I am beyond that

I have never left you
I have tried to run away
But inside I can't leave you behind
This is for you

Glorify

Glorify mornings
When I can see
No sound is heard
And the world sleeps away
Glorify mornings
Everyone, so it seems
Is still
No arguing, quarrel is halted.

Ode to a Secord Chance

I don't like people telling me what to do
Stopping me from doing what I want
Keeping me from being happy
I don't like people trying to sugar-coat everything
To meet their "right" life purpose
Or "correct" philosophy for what life is about.
Speak for yourself
Use history and proof if you want
But don't put me in a box
Don't have me be somebody I can't be
Inspire
Persuade
I should have my own ideas
Am I able to take criticism?
Like somebody spoke adversely to my action
Just leave me alone, I'll make it right
Criticize the ocean and skies
Leave me alone though
Stay away
If you outnumber, I will avoid you
If you don't leave an outlet, how can I be free?
Follow the good, the love, the best instead
Separate real from non-reality
Wonder and create and share
For those who will care
You have an audience out there
Live the way you know
How you can
Where you can
The answer is yes to a second chance

Without a Sound

Run from noise
Not another machine
Digging
Grinding
Gasoline
Bring me to peace and quiet
Slow down improvement of the earth
For a moment
I know you need work
I know you have the payment to make
Improving the world can be done without a sound
Anonymously found
Like giving ice cream to the two in the corner
Ice cream from the maître d'hôtel
To who?
You don't even know
They will remember the gift
They won't remember you
Generosity begets generosity
"Pay it forward" you may not forego

Breathe

We work and work
It's what we do
Not who we are, but near
Hurry
This is my life here
Save and save
Just run them over or up the wall
Compete, be thankful, stay on track
Do your best, be excellent, just for today
Come back tomorrow and keep it steady
Remember to stay healthy
Resources are scarce so I take the bus
You can drive the Maserati
Unless I am old enough
And safe

Northwestern Summer

A summer
A season for thriving
A season for success
What worked was the timing
Did I really want to work?
Or just the position
Among the competition
I'll let you know
The flexibility
Among the scheduled majority
I never knew what I was doing
Before it was too late
And the summer was gone
Frozen over like a glacier lake
I remain with one question:
Am I fishing like the old days?
Not the same as: "Do you fish?"
Don't you know?
My final answer was "No not really"
And the season passed subtly
Until it remained no more
I learned more than I needed to know
A different place to fish and a reason to go
I'll leave you with this
Don't forget to be free
When you have the time
Just go outside
See you on the river
Where the water is cold
Until then, I hope you stay till you're old

Fantasy

In giving up everything
Even dignity and composure
She wishes she did not have to.
In telling the truth
Starting with herself
She wanders away
Whenever she gets nervous.
Her hope for our connection
Is like a flicker
It mostly goes out.
She wishes it never would
She knows about respect
She knows about manners
I could use some lessons I know
She really wants to change and grow
She changes over many years
Has not always been this way
Felt haphazard with my words today
Spoken out of insecurity
Rather than confidence.
Has not always been this way
Some days she is happy
Other days the weather takes a toll.
She looks up toward brighter days
On the inside, she steers until she grows old
She never will I am told.

Good News

What would good news sound like tonight?
A chair
A light
A quiet flight
What would good news sound like tonight?
Peace from above
No hurdle, no shove
What would good news sound like tonight?
A warm welcome
Cold glass of stout
What would good news sound like tonight?
No hard stares
Only those who care
About you
You may not care about them
And they may care about others more
But they will and they do
What would good news sound like tonight?
If all were made right, and you wouldn't be hurt anymore.

Mood

The mood that I'm in
If all you're going to do is comment
Don't even show up
Skylights above
The mood that I carry
If all I can do
Is cry and cry
Skyward blue
I made a comment
Maybe I was baited
Others will do the same to me I am sure
As time goes on
Personally jaded
The way I look is never the way I feel
Maybe I should back down some
But hold on to some love
In the back of the corner
In the back of my mind
At least they don't say
I look too uncommon
At least not yet
Save us from your fears
From being too angry
To too many tears
At least not yet
I ain't so sure about it
Get out of the way
Get out of the way

Slow Tsunami

How to survive a slow tsunami
Slow over many miles
Intended to uproot
And destroy
But natural
Like the oceans of the earth
Here today
Tomorrow calm
You can have your way: calm
I will accept the delayed luggage
From an intended intimidation
An epic wielding of storied power
But I yield, that's what is needed
To the slow Tsunami
No other choice
And I bear down and only hope to survive
For as long as possible
Save me from the time of trial
And from those who want my neck
From the gentle correctors
From the people with weapons
Slow me from your tempest
There is a party at the beach
And I was not invited to sleep

Nova

I remember
You were encountered
Many, many years ago
Maybe in December
Maybe in July
All came together
Just to say hello
Break down the rhythm
Take it to the house
Not far off
But we were very young
No idea
Too new
To the way of the rhythm
And a sound from inside
Stand up to the front
Get away from me
Shout a melody
I can't seem to stop you
Those days are long gone
What we had never wrong
New days of nova straight up ahead
New sound and rhythm
Moving through our heads
Carried from a new day
Pull me, I'll be led

World Spin

Spinning my life
Spinning my days
Spinning my nights
You are always beside
You teach me how to speak
But not too wild
Far away from you, I often wander
Always dancing back
To where I come from
As if the world is round
Yes, I need to return
No, I needn't go out again
Too much movement and glide
Stop me from spinning through the night

Softer

Holds great design work
Great at all the detail
Knows what it's like
To fit it all together
Never a miss
Never chose to play around
But did it out of charity
For free
You may be an angel to me
Heaven's eyes
I may be blind
You helped me see
Through sound
I still should not ask
You to move
Nor should I question your devotion
Your faith is your own
It's all yours
Stop me from stealing
What is yours
But you are
All that is yours
I am old enough
To know better
But I am pulled in
From the weather
Toward your softer words of shelter

Unlimit

Sunlight
Sky is the limit they say
From earth to infinity and beyond
What does it sound like?
Sunlight I'm on the earth today

Sunlight where is your limit?
Where do you come from?
Streetlight where is your stare down?
I am standing up right now on earth with you.

I decided to break free
on my own, like you
Leaving my troubles behind
Only to warm someone else
Without you, I would be nothing

Come Back, Friend

I am bound to go out just to wander into you
It's not that I think about you so much
It is only on my better days, it all surfaces
You know where I fall
It has been years, oh.
You were always outside
New, saving me from ruin
You must be older too
Your image brings in a good way
To ask: will I ever see you a second day?
Or someone else similar?
You sobered me awake
Only to leave a lasting impression
I was wrong or too careful
God help me say to you the words
Don't make me late again
I didn't even know who you were
And I never stop wondering
Where you came from
What you wanted to say
I did not wait long enough
Where did you go?
With no sound?
Gone.

They Need You, Not Me

They need you, not me
I am a stranger to them
Not to be rude, but
It's true
They trust you
With everything
With their lives
Over time
I am only foreign
To their formality
Your sound makes sense
Let me move on
From your conquering
You win
As for me and my confidence
I am humbled yet sad
Will there be another day?
Or is this how I will go out?
Let me be without a doubt
Of my value
Not to you
But to everyone else
I guess I start to really wonder
Where my value rests
Not in your house
But with another Guest
With whom I am forgiven

Basement

Do I think too much?
Do I think about too much too fast?
Yoga, he says
His solution was yoga
I think about too much of the world
Too many things
All at the same time
Creates worry
I start thinking too much
Too many things to worry about
Too much information
Just want to be safe
Able to sleep
Able to do what I want to do
Travel, be healthy
Spread joy
Just reducing pain or helping to
Went to an old house one day
Way up north
Basement
Dirty, built before my time
Not a big house
Not really kept up too well
Kind of smelled bad
Smelled like whoever was living there
Was starting to deteriorate or something
And man, it smelled bad
So, I didn't stay too long in that house
Felt like it needed some work
Some fixer-upper work

Kind of familiar
Maybe I am just like that old house
I don't know. maybe
So how do you "fix up" yourself on the inside?
Maybe some of the old stuff goes
And the new stuff comes in
Newer stuff
And there is a lot of newer stuff that needs to come in
From the basement to the second floor

Look up

What do you do
When you feel like a lot of people are mad at you?
Like they want to blame you
For everything?
Like there is nothing you can say
That is right or fixes things
All you seem to get is a pointing finger in your face
What do you do with that?
How do you get people off your back?
Humor, entertain?
Laugh stress and anger away
Does it work?
Who has perfect information?
Make peace
Get off my back
Please
Glad
Be happy
Be the bigger man
Humble
If you can

Under the Surface

Where there was no water
I found a rhythm from a river
You never said a word
I realized it too
You always stood there with me while I made it through
I don't know why I said the things I said
I know I must be in over my head
In something going on
Under the surface
Underneath the light
Let me check it out and get back to you
I didn't even listen to a word from you
And you were right there
You are still right there
I guess I got in over my head again
And I know where I should go but
Maybe I wanted to test and push the limits
Of who I am
And where I stand
I am human
And I need more than my own words to survive
In the deep end away from the boat
Total stranger Let me float
Total stranger Let me float
Is it ok to be out of control?
What's going on under the surface?
Is it peace-making?
Don't let the sun go down, don't let the sun go down

Going to Tahoe

Plan to head out to Reno
All the way from the east coast
Man, have I got a ways to go
I want to see and ski Tahoe
I know you love the big snow
The big show on the snowboard
Downhill all the way from the lift
I believe you will make it all fit
In the calendar
On the schedule
I am headed out west
To be there right away
My goal
I need to count up the savings
Make sure I can make it work
All the way out to Reno
Drive me to the airport in the morning
I promise no scorning
Or little to no snoring
Just say you will go with me
And tell the sky to be clear too
So we can see the night stars

Meshing of the Days

Sleepless
At least for three days
Restless
And busy all the same
Argue
I can't seem to stop us
Quiet
Find me in the morning
Head and back
Relax
Chest and knee
Be free
For tonight I am coming home
Carry me to bed
Tuck me in
Leave a light on
Open a window
Separate tomorrow from today
Help me to remember
What's most important
And close the door when you go

Reconcile

Haven't seen you in a while
It has been a long time
Good to hear from you
Never thought I would run into you
Nice to see you
I heard good things too
You thought I forgot about you
You thought I ran out on you
Never would in a million years
They always say
You are never alone
Better to collaborate
The more the merrier
That's where I find myself
Looking you up
Now, where did we leave off?

Attention

I am here for you
I know you
I've never heard enough
Tell me more
I am here for you
I've never kept track
I've never looked back
Tell me more
About you
Just want to know more
I want to talk more
I need to feel grounded
With where you are
Express only the truth
What would we do without it?
Can't get enough of it
And I hear whatever you have to say
Compare me to no one
And save me from another's attention

If All I Can Do

If all I can do is write
I choose to write about us
If my body ages
And my talents slowly begin to fade
I shall move forward with you in mind
How you have put in so much time
On my behalf
More than I know
And more than I will ever understand
I've tried to work hard but my efforts often fall short
I believe I know where I need to be
And I don't want to ride anyone's coattails
Or live someone else's dream
But with you, there is always time
Our time
The time we have left, the time we spend
Valuable like water
Essential like the sun
And I will go on with not just anyone

Vision

One day I will go
To the undeveloped country
To the fields of old age
Filled with mountains, rivers, and sage
For only one reason: to retire
Some never plan nor aspire
Retiring is overrated
So, I was told
Hurry evaporates
Quiet emerges
Peace rests upon one human soul
For the rest of my days
I don't plan to retire alone
Near a town with a few dwellers
Have a few folks to talk to
Every now and then
I imagine
Loneliness could sweep in
If I let it
One lesson I learned
I'll never forget it
It is tough for a man to truly feel earned
Only with the sound of a river
A few words
And plenty of mountains
In the background
Will he finally rest his soul

Love Until You Can't

Every day begs me to love
Someone will need it
Another can't receive it
But here I am for both
Without expecting return
Willing the best for another
As other
Is to love
If I only love those who love me
What good will I be
To anyone
Like spinning wheels in the sand
Like a broken record of a rock band
Like a leaky hose cracked and too old to hold water
My neighbor loved by offering to help me
It's ok to do the same
Even if he doesn't know my name
One day my neighbor will be gone
Or I will have left
It's more than just getting along
It is a quest to love
Love until you can't
Until you are entirely spent

Gift

He takes time with it
Doesn't say anything just yet
Holds it
He wants her to say it's not enough
He wants her to take it back
Or give it away
It's what he feels
And it's what he wants to give
Just wanted to give it to her
Slowly she moves to understand
It matters if she likes it
Not he
And she smiles

Memory

Older
Fatter
More wrinkles, more freckles
Today is everything
Tomorrow the exterior
Fades
Memory remains
I forgot to ask could we go back to youth again?
Closer, closer we race toward our eternal end
To the great unknown
Aging and memory
Racing faster to relate
Looking back only to remember your voice
And how I was star struck
At such a young age
Your timing was perfect
But it was only once and gone
And you remain a memory only
I still reach out to you
But it's only from a memory
A glance or a glimpse only for a memory
And I will you to be extraordinarily happy

Homeward

I long for an embrace
A hug, a smile, a firm handshake
Something I must have missed for many months
Travel and tour wears down a soul
You start to wonder if a home is still your end goal
From where you started it seems like forever ago
Home
A place where you can go
A place where you need to go
A place where you belong
Or are you marching to a new song?
A wanderer's anthem?
If I can still make it there am I welcomed?
And will I be well-rested when I get there?
Days lengthen, travelers strengthen
Only to find their way back home
That's how I am I guess: need me a place to rest
A real home
Is that too much to ask?
A home has really been my only task
Since I first left
Peace and quiet lead me back
To where you first welcomed me and to where I am destined to return

Rough Out There

They tell me life is hard
Rough out there
Or, I am supposed to think it's unfair
Life
You just like it or leave it
Believe it or be deceived
Kind of makes me sad
Or makes me wonder about one's life
The value of one's life cannot be fathomed
Or measured like a chasm
But worth even more in my book
One life, stolen away like a glance or a look
In a moment
Unfair or beautifully generous
It's only when you try to hold it
Or when you try to control it
That it freely bounds away
And you want it to stay and stay
But there it goes
Summoned roughly away

Generosity

Oh, to breathe pure air again
Only pure air with lots of oxygen
No smog or fog, just a breath of air
Give and give your voice when you have the time
I will listen and hear and take time for us
It's what I enjoy most: our company of peaceful love
Share what you must, at your discretion and I will listen
While we take the time out of time
No need to hurry, I have plenty of moments for you beyond our today
Generosity
Finally, we set another day apart like a Sabbath song of rest once more
Let it be air for our lungs forevermore

Down a Waterslide

I climbed a tower at just the right hour
Gravity took care of the rest
Feet backward and head first
I launched down the ride of my life on my chest
Twisting and turning with water pouring beneath
Faster and faster at greater and greater speeds
Until the ride broke and I plunged into a pool below
Swimming and bobbing I began to slow
What a ride down a waterslide
Again, I must go

Inspire

Pay attention to your emotion
Close attention without division
Of mind and heart
Of who you are
Learning to say less
Might bring out the best
Action without reaction, without a test
When a flame is lit, it will go and go
Burn brighter and longer until it starts to slow
All that's needed is a spark
A life with another listening from the start
To the will to go on with desire
Through your words, you will continue to inspire

Don't Start with Me Then

If you are going to leave, don't call me
If you want to break my heart
Or tell us apart, or even cut me off
Don't start with me
We won't have to be together
For you to walk away forever
Just connected in some lighter way
Like on the telephone
Like on the movie screen
You know within the first conversation it seems
Within a few seconds
No, then don't start with me
If you are going to leave
Be clear and go slow
Just don't start with me if you're going to go
If you are not all in, if you know you mean a lot
If you are calling again
Just don't start with me then

Hard to Believe

You act like you love everything about me
Hard to believe
Never felt like this
Will this last?
Won't you grow tired and weary?
I had to ask

I know I act as though I don't care about anything
But you know that's not true
It's tough to express every day how much I care about you
I won't sugar coat it or make it up
I won't fake it until it's all used up

It's only for you though
Granted, enough time has passed for you to already know
Nothing can be hidden when enough light shines for one
Walk with me through the day and never leave me all alone

Camera, Lights, and Tears

Take me to the highland
Out of the wasteland
I'll send you my love
I'll send you my love
Oh, take me away

Take me to London
To the big, big city
Let's see the world
See Beijing and the east
Oh, take me away

The storms are too much
Don't say anything that would hurt me
Or give a face too sad and too tough
All put together

I will listen to you
I will hold on to you
Just take me away
Our home might be gone when we return
But I will still need you

Oh, love me
Take me away
Give me, give me your best
I won't put you down
Or put you up to the test

Your careless face is new
One day you will be here too
I'll send you my love
I'll send you my love
Don't forget

I used to sit here for hours on my own
Made me feel something
Like I was living to leave for someone
All my life for someone

If you are good you could see the world
We could go together
It would be fun she said
I am not made to rule the world

Only made to be next to you
I can only do so much
Rule me, rule me, run me
Just take me with you

Do you hear that?
New York was calling
Your name is better
It's all in there just don't forget me
I'll send you my love

Windsail

Open the door
Tear down the vertical walls
That so divide and contain you in

Organize and let up
Get up out of the valley
Climb out if you would and release

Honor the holy one by living free to love
Not feeling trapped or made up
Uncouple from the boxing gloves

When they want to condemn you
Remind them who you are
And always tell the truth as it pertains to you

Don't argue a beat, I won't argue with you
Don't argue with me, I won't argue with you
We won't argue anymore

Are you so afraid the truth will not be heard?
Are you so afraid you may not be heard anymore?

Open the door
Tear down the vertical walls
That so divide and contain you in

Organize and let up
Get up out of the valley
Climb out if you would and release

Tell

Tell me a story, make it a real one
Now, tell me now, tell me now, tell me now
What I need to know
Don't I deserve to know
Make it fit, make it real
Make it happen

What if I let go, wrote down what I could
Uncensored would it make sense to anybody
Or anyone down
Make it happen
Make it work
Now tell me now

Match me, make me a sound
Like I can listen to your story about
Being good and glorious all day long
Fully in need of no one

Hide me, hide me away from the evil one
The evil who seeks to scare me away
And take away my freedom
Tell me a story
Now make it real
Make it all about freedom

To Watch a Surfer

Sensation
Elation
Elaboration
Spin around, spin off the top, fly in the air
Only to reside behind the water
Catch another
I'm not going to ride that with you
It's your wave, know I see you
I'm not going to get too near you
It's your wave just know I see you
You're having an ocean carvation
In an ocean elation
An ocean sensation
You've got to be wise
I am by your side.
Sensation
Elation
Moonlight's tomorrow
Coordination, spin it around
In the ice-cold flood of ocean suds
Delayed gratification, moonlight tomorrow
Spin around
You're having an ocean carvation
In an ocean elation
An ocean sensation
You've got to be wise
I am by your side.

Candle, Flames, and Sound

Rock and roll
Rock and roll candle
Rock and roll
Rock and roll candle
Pop and tap
Keep moving through the soul
What did he say?
I will find a way
When the sun sets
And the moon brings a light
Find a way
Through movement of the soul
Tap, tap ring
Sleep and sleep
Ring and ring
Rock and roll
Rock and roll candle
Smells of incense to me

A New Year's Hope

So many people all hurrying throughout
Running and driving and hustling about
There's only space to breathe without getting run over
Get out of my way I'm important to another
Enjoy the weather if you might
Pay attention to everyone's plight
You aren't the only human alive don't you know
Coexist until you find a way to go
Out to the moon or maybe to Mars
Catch a ride on technology it will take you so far
Talent everyone has, it's all over
But not easy to get along with six billion shoulder to shoulder
Love, they say, drives away fear
Love is what I will hope for everyone in the new year

Bimini and Aging

For the first time, tides of the sea
I can feel aging taking over
Resting in a quiet chair on a sandy beach
My younger day runs into the waves without me
I try to understand but all she manages is a laugh
Not too loud and not at me, at least I don't think
But a laugh
Mocking my unknowing
My insecurity she laughs and laughs
One day I will be too old to go in
Aging again
No one asks it to stop
Aging again
Everyone participates except me
Do I want to go in?
Really, it is too cold and unfair
Or barely warm enough to go in slow
I decided to let youth fade away
I laughed too, and all I once knew
Is washed away in tides of ocean flume